Beyond the Ordinary Camera

Diane Bair and Pamela Wright

Contents

Rigby

Cameras Are Everywhere

"Smile!" "Say *cheese!*" Most of us have had our picture taken many times. We smile for the camera with our family, friends, teammates, and classmates. Perhaps you own a camera yourself. People use cameras every day to record special moments and events. When it comes to cameras, though, this is just part of the picture.

You may have had your picture taken several times today and were not even aware of it. Special cameras take pictures of us at the bank, at stores, perhaps even at school, or on the street corner. At this very moment, a camera attached to a **satellite** in space might be snapping photographs of your neighborhood. If you get hurt or become very ill, your doctor might use a tiny camera to look inside your body to see what is wrong.

In this book, we will look at several different types of cameras and the extraordinary ways people use them to get a closer look at our world and the universe.

35mm camera

video camera

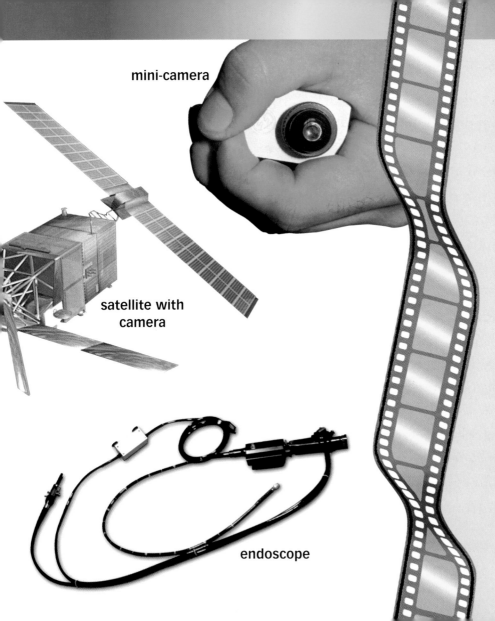

mini-camera

satellite with camera

endoscope

THE SCIENCE OF A PHOTOGRAPH

What really happens when you take a picture? It all has to do with light and chemistry. When you press the camera's button to take a photograph, a shutter is opened. While the shutter is open, light is reflected from the objects in front of the camera onto the film inside the camera. The film undergoes a chemical change when the light hits it. This chemical "recording" of the image makes a picture.

Crime-Stopping Cameras

You have probably seen lots of home videos. Perhaps someone in your family filmed your last birthday party or vacation.

Video cameras are fun to use, but they are also powerful crime-fighters. Many stores and businesses use video cameras to prevent shoplifting, or stealing. You may have noticed a small camera pointed toward you in a store, an elevator, or a bank. These cameras are on all the time. The images they take are sent through cables to a TV monitor at another location. Police officers or security officers watch the images.

The basic idea behind these video cameras is to reduce crime. People who know they'll be caught on film will be less likely to do something wrong. If someone actually *does* rob a store where there's a video camera, the robber may be identified by the film. When a camera is used this way, it's called a **surveillance** camera.

Photo taken by a surveillance camera in an art museum

HIGH-TECH VIDEO

When video cameras were first invented, they were big and bulky and the picture quality was not very good. The newest cameras are much better. The images are sharp. New technology makes it possible for pictures to be sent through cables or telephone lines to locations many miles away.

Some video cameras can turn in every direction. Some are equipped with heat-sensing devices, motion detectors, bulletproof cases, even small wipers in case rain or snow blurs their lenses. The newest video cameras are also much smaller than early versions. Tiny microchip cameras can be hidden easily.

Have you had your picture taken today? Think of all the places you've been—could there have been a camera pointed at you?

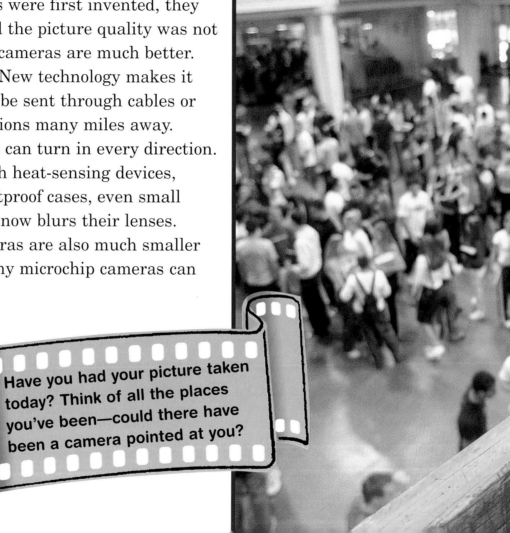

SAFE AT SCHOOL

Some schools have begun using surveillance cameras for the safety of their students, teachers, and school property. For example, schools often have expensive equipment, like computers, that is attractive to burglars. Using video cameras, school officials can keep an eye on school property even when school is closed.

Private detectives and police officers use surveillance cameras to take pictures of suspected criminals and collect evidence of crime. Often they use tiny, lightweight cameras, some as small as a quarter. Tiny cameras are easily hidden, and can be installed in a baseball cap, a watch, or even on a pair of sunglasses!

A student security officer videotapes high school students in a courtyard during lunch hour.

HIDDEN CAMERAS, PUBLIC PLACES

To cut down on crime, some communities have set up cameras in public places. Often the cameras are placed in neighborhoods where drug dealing and gang activity is a problem. Sometimes these cameras are hidden, and sometimes they are in plain sight. On street corners, in parks, in parking garages, and in subway stations, these cameras record the activities of people who come and go.

The images from the cameras are sent to TV monitors that are set up at a different location. Police officers watch the monitors. An officer who sees a crime in action quickly contacts the officers who are already in the area, describing the suspects to them. Those officers can then make a speedy arrest.

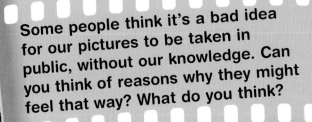

Some people think it's a bad idea for our pictures to be taken in public, without our knowledge. Can you think of reasons why they might feel that way? What do you think?

Satellite Cameras

Imagine a camera up in space that can take pictures of Earth so detailed that they show the difference between an oak tree and a pine tree. This kind of camera, called an **imaging satellite**, exists today. Imaging satellites are carried into space by space shuttles. While orbiting Earth, each satellite snaps pictures of selected areas with a **digital camera**. The pictures are sent to Earth and received at ground stations.

Imaging satellites are quite useful for observing the ever-changing weather here on Earth. Weather satellites photograph clouds and storms and provide information for weather stations. Based on the movement of the storms, scientists can predict weather conditions around the world.

I SPY, YOU SPY

Spy satellites were first used in the 1960s. By taking pictures from space and beaming them back to Earth, countries at war could take pictures of each other's military tanks and aircraft, weapon sites, and target zones. Now, new kinds of imaging satellites deliver sharper pictures. Even in peacetime, governments use these pictures to gather military information.

Satellite image of a hurricane off the coast of Florida

HOW A DIGITAL CAMERA WORKS

Digital cameras are sometimes called *filmless cameras.* Instead of using film, digital cameras change the image in the camera's view into computer code. A computer then translates the code back into a picture.

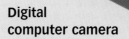

Digital computer camera

THE BIG PICTURE

People are always dreaming up other ways to use imaging satellites. Scientists use satellite pictures as a way of looking at our planet. By studying pictures of forests taken over time, researchers can see which kinds of trees are growing and how healthy the forest is. Satellite pictures also provide a sky-high view of cities, oceans, and crops. Volcanoes and other natural disasters can also be studied by satellites.

Satellite pictures provide an overview of the places where people and animals live, helping researchers who study population growth. In the future, satellite images might be used by farmers to check on crops, by fishing-boat captains to spot schools of fish, and by prospectors looking for oil, gas, and minerals.

Someday soon you might be able to buy pictures of your own home or your favorite vacation place that were photographed from space.

Did you know that anything that orbits Earth is called a *satellite*—even the moon? But most people use the word *satellite* to describe an object that is put into space for a specific purpose.

Infrared Photography

Some cameras do more than take a picture of what a person or an object looks like. These cameras can photograph light that can't be seen by your eyes. This is called **infrared imaging**.

An infrared camera can take pictures in total darkness. An infrared camera detects energy from an object, then changes that into a picture. The hotter and colder parts of an object show up as lighter and darker areas. If, for example, you took a picture of a black dog at midnight, the picture would show the dog's body in different colors. The warmest parts would appear red and yellow, while the coolest parts would look green and blue.

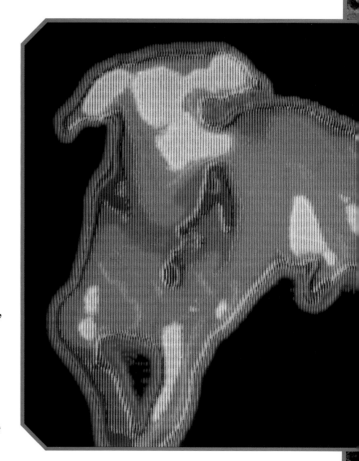

(right) An infrared photo of a dog
(far right) A firefighter is using thermal imaging to check for people trapped under a landslide.

WARM AND COOL IMAGES

As you might guess, infrared photography is used in some interesting ways. The U.S. Forest Service uses infrared pictures taken from airplanes to locate and track forest fires. Wildlife scientists use these pictures to count animals. The animals appear as bright spots of color in the dark woods. When people are lost in the wilderness, search-and-rescue crews use infrared cameras to help find them in the dark.

In Idaho, the U.S. Forest Service monitors the health of trees with infrared photography. Red trees are healthy and gray trees are dead.

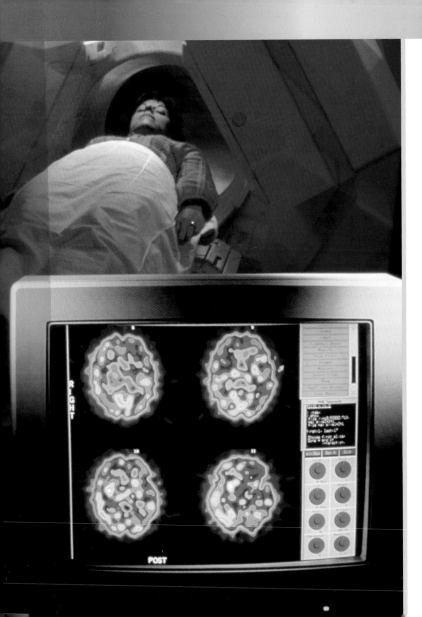

Veterinarians and ranchers also use infrared cameras to check on the health of their animals. Those that are sick or not eating well give off a cooler image than healthy ones.

For people, doctors use this imaging to identify medical problems like toothaches, migraine headaches, and nerve injuries. With infrared pictures, doctors can see through skin. They can see blood vessels easily and can detect diseases like cancer, too. Tumors show up like hot spots in infrared pictures.

REVEALING WHAT CAN'T BE SEEN

Researchers use infrared cameras to study documents that are very old or have been damaged and can no longer be read. Used this way, infrared imaging is a tool that can help solve age-old mysteries. It was used to reveal the ancient writing on the Dead Sea Scrolls—writing that was too faded to be visible to people.

Infrared photography can even help experts solve crimes. Infrared pictures can reveal signatures on written documents like wills or checks that were erased and written over. This technology can also reveal "fake" signatures on paintings. The camera can see what the human eye cannot.

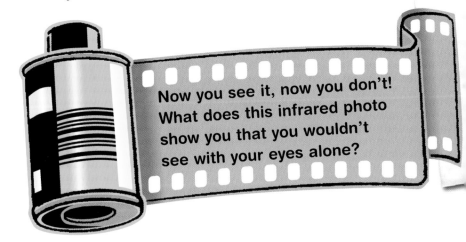

Now you see it, now you don't! What does this infrared photo show you that you wouldn't see with your eyes alone?

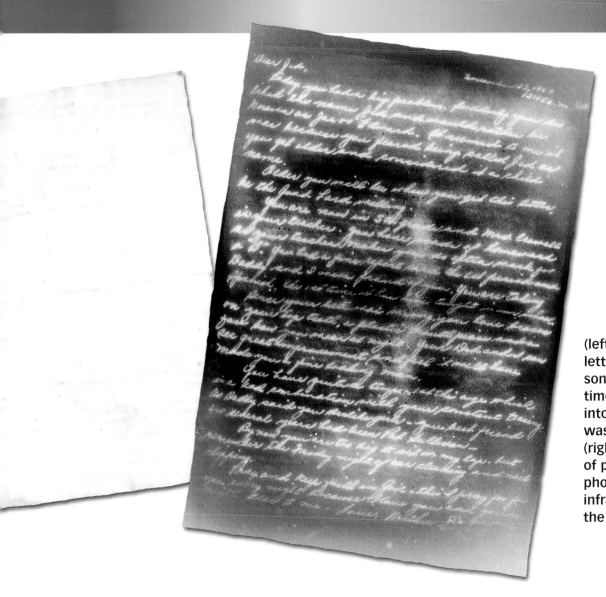

(left) A mother wrote a letter to her 5th grade son and placed it in a time capsule. Water got into the capsule and washed the ink away. (right) The same piece of paper was photographed with infrared film to reveal the letter.

Cameras Inside Your Body

Imagine being able to see inside your body—to watch your heart beat or look at the inner workings of your stomach. That's what doctors can do with a special camera device called an **endoscope**.

The endoscope is a long, thin tube with a tiny video camera and light on the end. The camera-carrying tube is as thin as a pencil's lead and no bigger than most food you swallow! The picture from the endoscope is then shown on a monitor.

Doctors use endoscopes to look for problems in your body that may require treatment. Also, by using an endoscope during surgery, doctors can make much smaller cuts in a patient's body than they did before. This helps the body heal much faster.

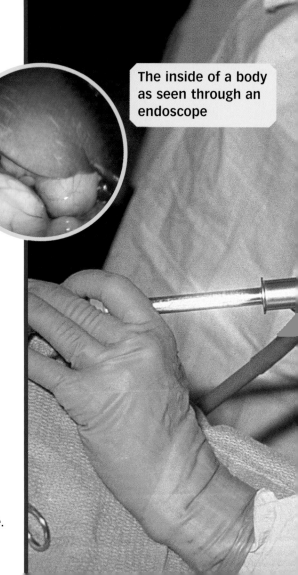

The inside of a body as seen through an endoscope

A surgeon photographs the inside of the body using an endoscope.

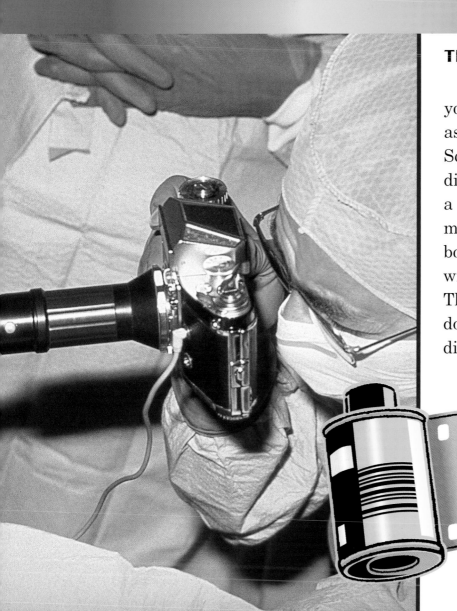

TIME FOR YOUR PILL

In the future, seeing inside your digestive system may be as simple as swallowing a pill. Scientists are now working on a dime-size capsule that contains a miniature camera. As the pill makes its journey through the body the same way food does, it will send signals to a computer. The new camera pill would allow doctors to see inside your entire digestive tract!

Can you think of other ways that doctors could use cameras?

OPEN WIDE!

Open wide and smile for the camera! Next time you sit in the dentist's chair, you may be watching a movie—starring the inside of your mouth. Some dentists use special cameras that are about the size of a pen when they examine your teeth. By watching a television screen in the examination room, you're able to see what the camera sees.

Soon dentists hope to use cameras to help clean teeth, too. A high-powered instrument will feature one of the world's smallest cameras. The camera will look deep inside the gums around the teeth. These pictures will give dentists magnified views of the area— up to 46 times larger than they'd see with the naked eye. This will help dentists find and remove hidden plaque that hurts your teeth and gums.

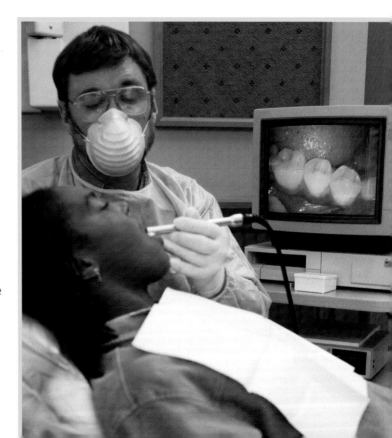

Microscopic and Telescopic Cameras

Would you like to see what a germ looks like? Cameras that photograph through microscopes reveal an awesome world hidden from the naked eye. These pictures are called **photomicrographs**. They can show things that have been magnified up to 20 million times!

Sometimes photomicrographs are used to teach students about science and to train doctors. Crime specialists may use them to find hidden clues. Some people take photomicrographs of gemstones, minerals, and even snowflakes, because they think the pictures are interesting and beautiful. What do you think?

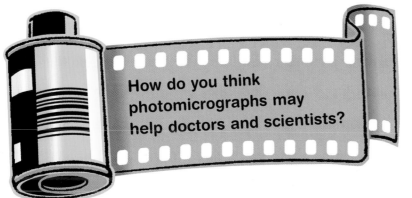

How do you think photomicrographs may help doctors and scientists?

These photomicrographs are of a gem called a garnet (top), a snowflake (middle), and a mineral called mica (bottom).

CAMERAS IN SPACE

Did you know that a telescope nearly the size of a large bus is whirling around Earth, taking pictures of planets and stars? The Hubble Space Telescope travels at five miles per second, completing one full orbit of Earth every 97 minutes. Along the way, the telescope sends pictures to scientists on Earth. Scientists study the pictures to learn new things about the universe.

MARS TO EARTH

NASA has sent several probes into space equipped with **telescopic cameras**. One of these, a spacecraft called Mars Global Surveyor, has been orbiting Mars and taking pictures since 1996. The pictures reveal some new things about this planet.

For many years, scientists thought that Mars was a very dry place. Now, new pictures of the planet show that many years ago, Mars may have had water on the ground in lakes and streams. This is just one way that the telescopic cameras on space probes are helping us solve the mysteries of the universe.

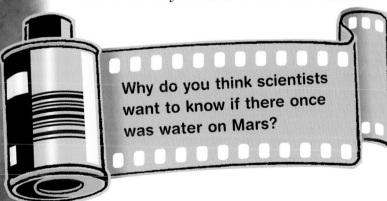

Why do you think scientists want to know if there once was water on Mars?

(far left) Hubble Space Telescope being put into orbit
(inset) Supernova photographed by Hubble Space Telescope
(right) Crater on Mars photographed by Mars Global Surveyor

Let Us Entertain You

Were his feet in-bounds when he caught the football? Did the puck go in the net? What a great play! Let's see it again! If you've ever watched a sporting event on television, you've probably seen an instant replay.

An instant replay lets us take a second look at something that just happened. It takes a lot of photographers to capture one instant replay picture. Several photographers shoot the action from different angles to be sure someone captures the right moment on film. These images are then sent to a television studio. An instant replay image is selected and shown to the audience— all within seconds!

In the past, sports replay systems used videotape similar to what you may play in your home VCR. Today, replays are created with digital computer technology. The new systems are quicker because there is no tape to rewind.

Initial action is filmed from two different angles.

Images are
transmitted via
satellite to the
television studio.

Instant replay image
is selected.

Instant replay is shown
to the audience.

GIANT PICTURES

Take one! If you've ever seen an IMAX® movie, you know how exciting it can be! These movies are made with extra-large cameras and extra-large film. The camera used can weigh up to 100 pounds and the film frame is ten times larger than the film that most people use in their cameras at home. The larger the film frame, the more information is on the film. This means the picture will be clearer.

IMAX movies are shown on giant screens, up to eight stories high, or on domes as large as 88 feet wide. The sound is not recorded on the camera. It is recorded on a special recorder with stereo sound. When you watch one of these movies, it feels like you are right in the middle of the action.

IMAX cameras have filmed extraordinary places and things. They have gone undersea to photograph the Titanic and to the top of Mt. Everest, the tallest mountain in the world. They have been flown into raging fires and spewing volcanoes to capture nature's fury. These cameras have even been carried on shuttle missions that have gone thousands of miles into space.

IMAX cameraman on Mt. Everest

A special IMAX camera has been installed at the International Space Station. The astronauts had to be trained to use the camera and handle the large reels of film.

What's Next?

Cameras are all around us. Some cameras are as big as a bus, others are as small as a quarter. Some cameras can take pictures in the dark. Some cameras take pictures of things too small to be seen with the human eye. Special cameras can even detect colors and light that are not visible to human beings.

Scientists continue to invent new and exciting ways to see the universe and solve its mysteries through the eye of a camera. Can you imagine what cameras will do next?

From top to bottom: (top) Camera scanning the retina of an eye for security; (middle) paper revealing a letter written from a mother to her son; (bottom) Volcano eruption. Gray area is ash covering the land.

Glossary

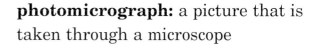

digital camera: a camera that takes pictures in computer code instead of on film

endoscope: long thin tube with a tiny video camera that doctors use to take pictures of the insides of their patients

imaging satellite: a camera that takes pictures from space of Earth, other planets, and stars

infrared imaging: photographing light that can't be seen by human eyes

photomicrograph: a picture that is taken through a microscope

satellite: an object that orbits the earth

surveillance: close watch kept over a person or object

telescopic camera: a camera that can take pictures of things that are miles and miles away

Index